Buster Cat Goes Out

By Joanna Cole
Illustrated by Rose Mary Berlin

A GOLDEN BOOK • NEW YORK
Western Publishing Company, Inc., Racine, Wisconsin 53404

Buster was a pretty orange cat who lived in a tall building with his friend Mr. Huggs.

Every night, when Mr. Huggs came home from work, he brought Buster's favorite catfood.

He scratched Buster in his favorite place—behind the ears.

And he played Buster's favorite game—chase-the-mouse. Buster was always happy when Mr. Huggs was home.

Every morning Mr. Huggs said, "Good-bye, Buster. Be a good watch cat today."

Then Mr. Huggs went out into the hallway. He got into a funny little room and pushed a button. The doors closed, and Mr. Huggs disappeared.

Buster always ran to the window and looked down. He saw Mr. Huggs walking up the street.

But Buster was very bored and lonely staying home all day by himself, so one day he decided to do something about it.

That morning Mr. Huggs said, "Be a good watch cat today," just as he always did. Then he went out the door, just as he always did. But this time Buster went, too!

Buster walked so quietly that Mr. Huggs did not even notice him. Buster hid behind an umbrella stand until Mr. Huggs got into the little room and went down.

After a few minutes, the doors of the little room opened again. Some people got out. Then, just before the doors closed, Buster ran in. He wanted to go down and walk up the street like Mr. Huggs.

But the little room did not go down. It went up!
Buster wondered what would happen.

When the little room stopped, the doors opened,
and Buster saw a terrible sight.

There in front of him stood a big growling dog.
Buster was scared. He growled back. Then the dog
showed Buster his big sharp teeth!

Luckily for Buster, the doors started to close
again. The dog jumped back, and the little room
went up!

When the doors opened again, there was a father and his little boy. The boy reached in and pulled Buster's tail. OUCH! Buster let out a yowl!

Luckily for Buster, the father said, "Be nice to the kitty."

The boy let go, the doors closed, and the little room went up again.

When the doors opened, Buster saw a big mean man with a broom. "Scat, cat!" said the man, and he tried to *sweep* Buster away.

"ME-OW-OW-OW!" Buster was mad! He would have scratched the mean man and his broom, but the doors closed too fast.

The little room went up again. It went up, up, up.
When the doors finally opened again, Buster
looked out. All around were green trees. Up above
was blue sky.

And straight ahead was a lady painting a picture.
The lady smiled at Buster. He liked her right away.

Buster climbed a tree halfway to the top. The
lady thought that was wonderful.

"What a strong little cat you are!" she said.

So Buster kept climbing, all the way to the top.
And the lady said, "Oh, no, that's too high!"

Buster looked down. For a minute he was a little scared. But then he found a good way to get down, and the lady said, "Aren't you smart!"

Buster found something square made of bricks. He wondered what it was, so he poked his head down inside to find out. When he came out, the lady thought a new *gray* cat had come to visit.

Then Buster washed himself, and she said, "Oh, it *is* you, after all!"

There were so many nice things to do that Buster
did not feel lonely or bored—not even for one
minute all day long!

At last the lady put away her painting things. She
and Buster went into the little room. This time it
went down, down, down.

When the doors opened, there was Mr. Huggs, just coming home from work.

"Buster!" said Mr. Huggs. "How did you get here?"

"He came to visit me on the rooftop today," said the lady. "He was good company!"

From then on, Buster was happy day *and* night. He stayed with Mr. Huggs at night, and he visited the lady during the day.

And everyone had beautiful paintings of Buster to enjoy!